MORE THAN A GAME

A STORY OF HEART, HOOPS AND FINDING YOUR VOICE

NEETU GURJAR

Contents

Acknowledgements

I would like to express my heartfelt gratitude to **The Sanskaar Valley School** for giving me the opportunity to write this book. A special thanks to my **English teacher**, whose guidance and encouragement helped shape my thoughts into words. I am also thankful to my parents, Coach Abhay, and my friends for always believing in me and supporting me through this journey.

Introduction

Basketball was never part of my plan. In fact, I stumbled into it by accident, just a curious sixth grader following her friends into a summer camp session. But what began as a random choice soon became a path filled with passion, sweat, and self discovery.

This book is not just about playing a sport. It's about what happens when a quiet girl, unsure of her place, finds her voice on the court. It's about long practices, missed classes, quiet disappointments, unexpected friendships, and the strength to keep going even when things don't go your way.

Through every chapter, you'll walk beside Aadhya, who might seem like just a character, but really, she is me. And maybe, just maybe, a little bit of you too.

This is my story, My journey

More than a game, it's where I found me.

ONE

THE UNEXPECTED PASS

It started with a summer camp.

The school corridors, usually silent in May, echoed with the buzz of students trying out new activities. Aadhya, who had signed up for cricket, the sport she loved most, found herself standing awkwardly in the basketball line instead.

The cricket camp had been cancelled. In its place was badminton, but that was full. With no other sport she really knew, Aadhya simply followed her two friends, Naira and Vivaan, into basketball. She had never held a basketball in her life. It felt foreign in her hands, like an invitation to a world she hadn't asked to enter.

The court was alive with energy. Balls bouncing, sneakers squeaking, kids practicing across the court. Aadhya stood off to the side, her fingers tight around the ball. She tried to mimic the dribbling she saw others doing—but the ball shot sideways and escaped.

Naira ran after it and passed it back with a grin. "Step one," she teased, "don't hold it like it's going to explode."

Vivaan chimed in, "Just bounce it once. We'll catch it if it runs away."

Aadhya laughed, half nervous, half grateful.

From the front of the court, a tall man with a whistle and asks everyone to form a line. The person was none other then Our mentor Abhay sir. separates everyone the beginners were asked to go to half court and the elite athletes were asked to go another half court.

Aadhya bounced the ball. It went sideways again and again Coach Abhay raised an eyebrow. "Try ten times. One for each doubt you had about being here.

And so, she did.

TWO

A SPARK IN MY SHOES

Aadhya's first few days in basketball were full of awkwardness. She had no idea how to dribble properly, let alone shoot a basket. The ball felt heavy in her hands, and every time she tried a shot, it either missed the hoop completely or barely grazed the rim.

But with each practice, Aadhya could feel something shifting. It wasn't just about getting the technique right—it was about the rush of the game, the rhythm of the court, and the rush of adrenaline that came with it. The sound of sneakers squeaking on the polished floor, the ball bouncing in a steady rhythm, and the energy of the players around her ignited a spark inside her.

She began staying after practice, asking Coach Abhay to help her fix her shooting form. Every time she tried a new drill, it didn't come easy. But every single time, Aadhya pushed herself harder.

The Struggle and the Support

Aadhya was struggling. She was putting in all her effort but still wasn't seeing the results she hoped for. After every practice, the bruises on her knees seemed to multiply, and she could feel the sweat pouring down her face. She knew she had to work harder, but it didn't make the sting of failure any less.

One day, after missing yet another shot during practice, Aadhya slammed the ball to the ground in frustration. The court was emptying out as most of the players headed home, but she stayed behind, feeling a lump in her throat.

"You, okay?" Vivaan asked as he stopped by her side, his voice soft. "You're pushing yourself too hard, Aadhya. You're gonna get it right—just keep trying."

Naira, who had stayed after practice too, gave Aadhya a reassuring smile. "You've got this, Aadhya. You're improving every day. Just think about how far you've come from the first time we met."

Those words were exactly what Aadhya needed. Despite the pain of missing shot after shot, Aadhya knew that Vivaan and Naira believed in her. It wasn't just the words they said—it was the way they showed up for her. Their support felt like a lifeline she didn't even realize she needed.

Coach Abhay, who had been watching from the sidelines, walked over to them. "You know," he began, his voice calm but steady, "every great player has been exactly where you are. The only difference between someone who succeeds and someone who gives up is how long they keep going when it gets tough."

Aadhya looked up at him, her eyes wide. "But Coach, it feels like I'm always failing."

Abhay nodded thoughtfully. "You're not failing, Aadhya. You're learning. And every failure is just a step closer to getting it right. Do you want to know the secret to success?"

Aadhya shook her head, eager to hear.

"Keep going. When the ball goes off course, when it feels like nothing is working, you try again. And again. And again. That's how you'll get better. You've already got the most important thing—you care. That's the hardest part."

The First Match: A Turning Point

It wasn't long before the school organized a practice match against another team. It was a small event, just for practice, but it felt huge to Aadhya. This was the moment she could show everything she'd learned.

During the match, she made mistakes—plenty of them. But she also made a few good passes and even managed to score a basket, the ball swooshing through the net with a satisfying swish. The roar of her teammates cheering for her felt like the best sound she'd ever heard.

Aadhya couldn't believe it. She had made it happen. She had pushed through the struggles, and this moment—this one shot—was proof that her hard work was paying off.

As the match went on, Aadhya grew more confident. Each time she missed a shot, she didn't beat herself up. She simply reset, got back into position, and tried again. The match was a game of constant ups and downs, but every pass, every dribble, every moment felt like progress. She wasn't just a beginner anymore. She was a player.

Her teammates—Vivaan, Naira, and others—cheered her on from the sidelines, but they didn't just cheer for her when she did well. They encouraged her when she missed a shot or got the ball stolen from her. "Nice try, Aadhya! Keep going!" Naira shouted.

Vivaan clapped his hands, "Don't stop now, you're doing awesome!"

And Coach Abhay? He was focused on Aadhya every step of the way, watching as she fought through every challenge. With every small victory, he gave a nod of approval, making her feel like every effort, no matter how small, was worth it.

The Moment of Realization

It was at that moment, as she dribbled the ball down the court, that Aadhya realized something important. Basketball wasn't just a game. It was a challenge, yes, but it was also a place where she could grow, find her voice, and build her confidence.

By the end of the match, Aadhya was out of breath, but her heart was racing in the best way possible. She hadn't won the game—at least, not on the scoreboard—but she had won something far more valuable: belief in herself.

And that, she realized, was just the beginning

THREE

A STAY BACK OF FRIENDSHIP AND GROWTH

It was winter, and stay backs were in full swing. The court was colder than usual, but Adhya didn't mind. She was getting better, faster, stronger, basketball was beginning to feel like home.

Summer camp ended, but Adhya's journey with basketball didn't. She enrolled in the school's basketball stay back program. Every afternoon after regular classes, she would stay behind while most kids rushed home. Her uniform swapped for her practice jersey, her school for sneakers with worn-out soles.

The basketball court became her second classroom.

She missed birthday parties, hobby classes, even some family outings. There were days she skipped snacks and went straight into drills. Coach Abhay Sir was strict, but never unfair. If someone was five minutes late, they'd run laps. if someone missed a pass, they'd redo the whole play. But Aadhya loved the structure. She was improving. Slowly, steadily. Her classmates started noticing. Some would ask her for help with passing techniques, others for tips on dribbling. They saw her dedication, and in turn, she saw their admiration. Her confidence grew with each practice session, each successful pass, and every basket made. During one of these stay backs, Aadhya made a new friend " Akhya ". She wasn't in the summer camp like others, but they were classmates. Akhya was little hesitant about basketball at first, but when she saw Aadhya practicing, she was a drawn to the game. Aadhya noticed her one day, standing on the sideline with a curious look. She wasn't sure if she should join in. Aadhya walked over, dribbling the ball between her legs.

"Hey" Aadhya said with a smile, "first time on the court?" akhya nodded shyly," Yeah , I've never played before. But I've been watching you and thought it looked fun."

Aadhya grinned. "It is fun. Want to give it a shot?"

From that moment akhya was part of the team. She wasn't as quick as Aadhya, but her determination to learn was unmatched. Day after day, they practiced together. Aadhya showed her how to dribble, pass, and shoot. Akhya struggled at first, but Aadhya encouraged her with every mistake, just like her friends had done with her.

One evening, after practice, Akhya turned to Aadhya, breathless but excited. "I'm starting to get the hang of it! My shots are getting better!"

Aadhya nodded, proud of her new friend. "you've got it. Just keep practicing."

Through the winter stay backs, their bond grew. They weren't just teammates, they were friends, each pushing the other to improve. Aadhya began to appreciate the game even more, not just for herself, but because she had someone to share it with.

But as all good things must come to an end, the winter stay backs finally wrapped up. The last practice session was filled with mixed emotions. Aadhya felt proud of how far she'd come, but the idea of no more daily practices made her heart sink. It had been a place of growth, a place of friendships, most importantly, a place where she'd learned more than just basketball.

As the winter stay backs came to an end, Aadhya and Akhya walked off the court together, both with a new sense of confidence. Aadhya knew that no matter what happened, basketball had become more than just sport for her, it had given her a friend, a teammate, and a place where she belonged.

The court might have been empty that day, but Aadhya's journey was far from over.

FOUR

BALANCE BETWEEN STUDY AND BASKETBALL

The winter sun was gentle, but Aadhya's schedule was anything but. Morning. began with hurried breakfast, school till afternoon, and then stay backs for

basketball. From there, she would rush to her coaching class, barely catching her breath, and still return home with books waiting and chapters to be completed. Most nights she studied till 2:00 AM, her eyes heavy, her back aching. She managed to keep up in class. But slowly, things started slipping.

Her marks began to drop.

She wasn't able to concentrate during lectures. Homework remained incomplete. And her teachers noticed.

It started one Monday morning.

"Aadhya, "her Maths teacher, Mrs. Arora, called after class, her voice calm but firm. "You've always been good at this. What's happening now?"

Aadhya stood quietly, looking down at her notebook filled with half-solved problems.

"I'm sorry, ma'am. I've been practicing a lot... for basketball. "Her voice cracked a little"

"Sports are important, "But not at the cost of your education. Balance is everything."

That same week, her English teacher, Miss Tara, asked her to stay back after a grammar test.

"Aadhya," she said gently, "this isn't you. You're capable of so much more. You haven't even written your assignments."

Aadhya nodded, tears welling up in her eyes. She felt as if she was letting everyone down, her teachers, her parents, even herself.

Then came the day that changed everything.

Her mother was called to school.

In the Principal's office, the teachers sat around with concerned expressions. One by one, they spoke about falling grades, incomplete work, and a student who was no longer the same in class.

"she's doing well in basketball, yes, "Mrs. Arora added, "But her focus in academics has nearly vanished. We suggest she skips the stay backs for now."

Her mother nodded slowly. "Honestly, I've been thinking the same. Her schedule is so fixed, school, stay back, coaching and then practices. She barely sleeps. And she studies till 2 in the morning. I'm worried too,"

That evening at home was quiet.

Her mother didn't scold her. She sat beside her gently and said,

"Beta, I see how hard you're trying. But if something is costing your health and future, we need to pause and rethink. I know how much basketball means to you, but your studies matter too."

Aadhya didn't argue. She knew they were right. But her heart was heavy.

That night, she lay in bed, staring at ceiling. All her efforts...were they not enough?

But just as she was about to give up, she remembered the words of coach Abhay, spoken week ago during cold winter practice.

"Success don't come from always winning. It comes from showing up, even when things feel impossible."

She wasn't going to quit. She made changes. She cut down on some coaching. She created a study timetable. She asked her teachers for extra help. slowly, began! To balance things.

Her friends, Vivaan and Naira, stood by her side.

They would help her revise notes during breaks, quiz her before exams, and remind her to eat something before practice.

"You're not alone in this," Naira said once, handing her a sandwich before stay back. "you've come too far to fall now,"

Vivaan added.

There were still hard days, but Aadhya was learning how to fight for both her dreams and her responsibilities. She knew now, basketball wasn't just about playing. It was about discipline, time, commitment. It was about rising every time you fall.

This chapter of her life had taught her what most people take years to learn. And she wasn't done yet.

FIVE

MORE THAN A GAME

But Adhya didn't quit

She adjusted She studied harder, found smarter ways to revise, and slowly pulled her grades back up. She knew if she had to play, she had to balance it all. It wasn't easy, but she didn't expect it to be. Even though She wasn't on the interschool team, something unexpected happened.

Coach Abhay began asking her to demonstrate drills.

She didn't get to the chance to wear the jersey, but she got something else. She was teaching the team players some of her moves. She helped fix their footwork, corrected their passes. It was subtle, but powerful. They listened to her.

One evening, while she practiced alone, a voice broke her focus.

"Hi..... can you teach me that move?"

It was a younger student, maybe in class 5, holding a basketball too big for her hands.

Aadhya smiled. " sure. Let's start with your grip."

She saw herself in that little girl, eager, nervous, curious. And for the first time, She realized something. She may not have the title. But She had the impact.

She still looked forward to being on the team one day. Her goal hadn't faded, it hadst deepened. Because now she knew, Basketball wasn't just a sport.

It was her emotion.

It was her place of confidence

A girl who never had the courage to even play a sport was not leading others, helping them grow.

Basketball taught her that. It wasn't just a game for her.

Let's wish her luck.

She may not have medal yet, but she has something far stronger.

She has herself.